"Look in your pocket," Orson said.

Nancy reached in and pulled out a slimy rubber tarantula. "Gross," she said. "That thing was in the same pocket as my banana taffy."

"Make sure Orson didn't leave any more yucky things in your pocket," Jessie said.

Nancy carefully dipped her hand into her pocket again. There were no more creepy crawlies. But then Nancy noticed something even more scary.

"Oh, no!" Nancy gasped.

"What is it, Nancy?" George asked.

"The taffy is missing," Nancy said. "And so are the passes!"

**The Nancy Drew Notebooks**

Available from MINSTREL Books

# THE
# NANCY DREW
# NOTEBOOKS®

#25

*Dare at the Fair*

CAROLYN KEENE
ILLUSTRATED BY ANTHONY ACCARDO

A
MINSTREL®
BOOK

Published by POCKET BOOKS
New York   London   Toronto   Sydney   Tokyo   Singapore

A MINSTREL PAPERBACK *Original*

A Minstrel Book published by
POCKET BOOKS, a division of Simon & Schuster Inc.
1230 Avenue of the Americas, New York, NY 10020

Copyright © 1998 by Simon & Schuster Inc.
Produced by Mega-Books, Inc.

ISBN: 0-671-00820-X

First Minstrel Books printing July 1998

10  9  8  7  6  5  4  3  2  1

Cover art by Joanie Schwarz

Printed in the U.S.A.

# 1

# Big Thrills . . . and Chills

**I**'ve been waiting all year for this day!" Eight-year-old Nancy Drew was standing at the entrance to Big Thrills Fun Fair.

"Wouldn't it be cool if Big Thrills was open even in the winter?" Bess Marvin asked.

"Sure," George Fayne said. "If you're a polar bear."

"Then the roller coaster would be a *polar* coaster," Nancy said with a giggle.

Bess and George were cousins. They were also Nancy's two best friends.

They were all together for the most exciting Saturday of the year. It was the day that Big Thrills opened for the season.

"I still can't believe Jessie is getting us passes to get in free for the whole week," Nancy said.

"Seven days of total fun!" George said. She pointed two thumbs up.

Jessie Shapiro was in the same third-grade class as Nancy, Bess, and George. Her mother worked at Big Thrills. Mrs. Shapiro was able to get passes for Jessie and her friends.

"Guess what?" Jessie called as she ran over from the ticket window. "My mom is getting the passes right now."

"Super!" Nancy cried. She brushed her reddish blond bangs from her eyes.

"Why aren't you giving a pass to Rebecca Ramirez, Jessie?" Bess asked. "Isn't she your best friend?"

"Rebecca *was* my best friend—until last Sunday," Jessie said. "That's when she took Amara Shane on a family picnic instead of me."

"Did you talk to Rebecca about it?" Nancy asked Jessie.

"I don't ever want to speak to Rebecca again," Jessie said.

"Well," Nancy said, "it's too bad you two had a fight."

"Yeah," George said. "But I'm sure glad you picked us for the free tickets."

Nancy stood on her toes and tried to peek over the Big Thrills gate. "I can't wait to see Coconut," she said.

Bess wrinkled her nose. "Who?"

"Coconut the Peekaboo Chimp," Nancy explained. "He sneaks up behind kids, put his hands over their eyes, and says—"

"Peekaboo!" Jessie laughed.

"Eeeww!" Bess said. "He probably has hairy knuckles and banana breath."

Just then Mrs. Shapiro walked over to the girls. She waved four pieces of paper in her hand. "Here they are," she announced.

"Way to go, Mom!" Jessie cried as her mother handed out the passes.

"Thank you," Nancy, Bess, and George said almost at the same time.

Nancy held her pass carefully. She loved the way it looked. It was pink with an orange border. The border matched the lining of her red jacket. On the pass were printed the words "Saturday to Saturday."

The girls waved their passes proudly as they followed Mrs. Shapiro through the front gate of Big Thrills.

"Awesome!" Nancy gasped once they were inside. "It looks even better than last year."

Everywhere Nancy and her friends looked there were rides. High in the sky was a Ferris wheel with colorful butterfly chairs. Another ride looked like a pirate ship rocking on a giant wave.

"Remember, girls," Mrs. Shapiro said. "The passes cannot be replaced. So take good care of them."

"We will, Mom," Jessie promised.

"Good," Mrs. Shapiro said. She checked her watch. "We'll all meet right here at this spot in two hours. I'll drive everyone home." Then she hurried away to her job at the Big Thrills office.

"Let's put our passes in a safe place," Nancy suggested.

"Good idea," Jessie said. She slipped her pass inside her red waist-pack.

"My jacket has huge pockets," Nancy told Bess and George. "I can hold your passes with mine."

"Okay," Bess said as she handed her pass to Nancy.

Nancy slipped the three passes into the right-hand pocket of her jacket.

"Button the flap on your pocket," George said.

"This isn't a real flap," Nancy said. "It's just for decoration." She patted her jacket pocket. "But the passes are safe in here."

"Guard them with your life," George said.

"She will," Bess said with a laugh. "Detectives don't lose things. They *find* things."

Nancy smiled. Everyone knew she

was the best detective at Carl Sandburg Elementary School. She had a blue detective notebook in which she wrote down all her clues.

"Okay, gang," Jessie said. "Which ride should we go on first?"

Bess jumped up and down. "How about the Doodle Duck? It has rubber duck boats that float on water."

"Rubber ducks? It sounds like a giant bathtub," George said.

"How about the carousel?" Nancy asked.

Before her friends could answer, Nancy heard a loud rumbling sound.

Uh-oh, Nancy thought. That rumble could mean only one thing.

"The Rambling Rosie!" Jessie cried.

The Rambling Rosie was the fastest ride at Big Thrills. It was the biggest roller coaster for miles around. And it was Nancy's least favorite ride.

A line was already forming when the four friends reached the entrance to the ride.

"Oh, great," Bess said. She pointed

to a wooden sign. It read, You must be as tall as this sign to go on this ride.

George shrugged her shoulders. "You're still too short, Bess."

"But I grew a whole inch since last year," Bess said.

"I'll keep you company, Bess," Nancy told her. "I'm not going on, either."

"Why not, Nancy?" George asked. "Last year the Rambling Rosie was great."

"Yeah," Jessie said. "It even flipped upside down."

Nancy made a face. "So did my stomach," she said.

George grinned. "You probably felt sick because of all the cotton candy we ate right before the ride. Remember?"

"Maybe next year," Nancy said.

"Okay," Jessie said. "Let's all meet at the carousel in half an hour."

Nancy watched George and Jessie run for the line.

"Who needs the Rambling Rosie, anyway?" Bess said. She adjusted her

pink scrunchie. "It would just mess up our hair."

"I have an idea," Nancy said. "Let's buy some taffy from Tony's Taffy Stand."

Tony was at Big Thrills every summer. He made taffy in many different flavors.

"I wonder what new flavors Tony has this year," Bess said.

Nancy began to giggle. "How about . . . pepperoni pizza?"

"Pepperoni pizza? Yuck-o!" Bess cried. "That would make me sick."

Tony's Taffy Stand was right next to the bobsled ride. Bess bought a small bag of strawberry-flavored taffy. Nancy chose banana.

Nancy ate a piece of taffy. Then she put the bag in her right-hand pocket.

"I'd better go easy on the candy," Nancy said. "I don't want to get sick again."

Nancy and Bess walked through the fair. They saw a large crowd standing in front of a stage.

"I wonder what's going on," Bess said.

Just then a man wearing a silver cape burst out from behind a red velvet curtain.

"It's Marv the Marvelous Magician," Nancy said. "He's here every summer."

"Mmmph," Bess said. She was still chewing her taffy. "Iwikemarph awot."

"For my next trick, I'll need an assistant from the audience," Marv said.

Nancy's hand shot up. Then she heard someone shout, "Out of my way!"

A boy with black hair pushed his way in front of Nancy.

"Orson Wong!" Nancy said. Orson was in their class.

"Ooh! Ooh! Pick me! Pick me! *Please!*" he called.

Orson was shouting so loudly that Nancy covered her ears. "Oh, well." Nancy sighed. "Maybe Orson should get picked. He *does* want to be a magician when he grows up."

"*If* he ever grows up," Bess said.

Marv pointed to Orson. "There's a kid who loves magic. Step right up, young man."

"Cool!" Orson cried. He pushed his way through the crowd. Marv helped him jump up onto the stage.

"Should we watch Orson help Marv?" Nancy asked Bess. "Or do you want to ride on the carousel?"

Orson made a goofy-looking face at the crowd.

Nancy and Bess looked at each other. "The carousel!" they said together.

On their way to the carousel, Bess grabbed Nancy's arm.

"Nancy, look," Bess whispered. "It's the creepy House of Screams."

Nancy shivered. "Check out the broken shutters and all the cobwebs."

"I wouldn't go in there if you did my homework for a year," Bess said.

"It can't really be haunted," Nancy said. "Can it?"

Bess began to whisper. "I heard that a werewolf lives inside. All year 'round!"

"A werewolf?" Nancy asked.

Bess nodded. "With long, dripping fangs . . . and hairy claws!"

Suddenly two hands covered Nancy's eyes. She reached up. The hands were fuzzy—and very, very hairy.

"Werewolf?" Nancy gulped. Then she screamed. "Somebody help me!"

# 2

# Poof!
# They're Gone

**O**oh, ooh, ooh!" a voice whooped in Nancy's ear.

The fuzzy hands came down, and Nancy whirled around. It wasn't a werewolf. It was a chimpanzee.

"Wow," Nancy said, "You must be Coconut the Peekaboo Chimp."

The chimp was exactly the same size as Nancy. He grinned at her. Nancy could see his big teeth.

Then Coconut reached into the pocket where Nancy had her taffy. But he quickly pulled his hand out when he saw a woman walking toward Nancy.

She was dressed in a tan pants suit and a straw hat.

"That's right, young lady," she said. "I'm Barbara Woodhall. I'm Coconut's trainer," the woman said. "And you are the first Peekaboo Pal of the day."

Bess waved her hands at Coconut. "Shoo, shoo! Go away!"

"It's okay, Bess," Nancy said. She shook Coconut's hand. "Coconut is very friendly."

Barbara Woodhall pinned a Peekaboo Pal button on Nancy's jacket. The button had a picture of Coconut on it. Then Ms. Woodhall took a banana from her backpack and gave it to Coconut. Coconut shrieked happily.

"Coconut will do anything for a banana," Ms. Woodhall said. "Next to taffy, it's his favorite treat."

Bess clutched her bag of strawberry taffy tightly in her hand. "Taffy?" she gulped.

"Coconut is so well-behaved," Nancy said. She watched the chimp peel the banana.

"He wasn't always that way," Ms. Woodhall said. "He did some naughty things two years ago." She chuckled. "That's when I sent him to Colonel Cafferty's School for Chimps. It was time he learned some manners."

Nancy watched Coconut finish his banana. Then he put the banana peel in the large pocket of his overalls.

"See?" Ms. Woodhall said. "Most monkeys would toss the banana peel on the ground, but not Coconut." She patted Coconut on his head. "Good boy!"

Coconut clapped his hands.

"We have some rides to go on," Nancy said. "Thanks for the pin," she told Ms. Woodhall. "Bye, Coconut."

Nancy and Bess walked toward the carousel. Nancy ran for her favorite white horse.

Suddenly a girl with dark hair peeked out from behind a bright orange rooster.

"Rebecca Ramirez!" Nancy cried. Bess ran over to join them.

"Hi, Nancy. Hi, Bess," Rebecca said. "Is George here, too?"

Bess nodded. "She's with Jessie on the Rambling Rosie."

"Jessie never told me she was coming here today," Rebecca said.

Nancy thought that Rebecca looked upset.

"Not only is Jessie here," Bess said, "but she gave us free passes for a whole week. Isn't that neat?"

Uh-oh, Nancy thought.

"Did you say passes?" Rebecca asked. "You mean, you got in free?"

"Show her, Nancy," Bess said.

Nancy sighed. She pulled the passes halfway out of her pocket.

Rebecca stared at the passes. "First, Jessie doesn't speak to me for a whole week. And now this!"

I'd better cheer her up, Nancy thought. She pointed to a plastic ladybug purse strapped across Rebecca's chest.

"I love your purse, Rebecca," Nancy

said. She slipped the passes back into her pocket. "Do you like ladybugs?"

Rebecca nodded. "I love ladybugs. They're so pretty. And lucky, too."

A bell clanged three times.

"The ride is about to start," Nancy said.

"I want to ride the pink-and-white rabbit," Bess said.

Nancy tried to get up on the white horse. It was so tall that she had trouble climbing up.

"Let me help," Rebecca said. She came up behind Nancy. She put her hands around Nancy's waist and gave her a push up.

"Thanks," Nancy called down from the horse. But Rebecca was no longer on the carousel. She was running away.

"Hey, Rebecca!" Nancy called. "Aren't you going on the carousel?"

Rebecca didn't stop running. She didn't even turn around. She just kept running until she disappeared in the crowd.

That's strange, Nancy thought as the carousel began to turn.

When the ride was over, Jessie and George were waiting at the rail.

"Guess who we saw?" Bess asked. "Rebecca Ramirez."

"Rebecca's here?" Jessie asked.

"You'll never guess who else we saw," Nancy said quickly. "Coconut the Peekaboo Chimp."

"No way!" Jessie exclaimed.

"What's he like?" George asked.

Nancy tapped her pin. "Well, he has a real big smile."

"He's kind of weird," Bess said.

"Speaking of weird," George whispered, "look who's coming."

"Orson Wong!" Jessie groaned.

Orson was dressed in a silver cape. He waved a long, sparkly wand in the air. "Abraca-dokey, arti-chokey!" he said.

"Ha, ha," Nancy said. "Hi, Orson."

"You mean, Orson the Awesome," Orson said. He took a bow. "I'm Marv's assistant."

"We know that," Nancy said. "Bess and I were there when Marv picked you."

"Marv didn't pick me for just *one* trick," Orson said. "He asked me to be his assistant for the whole day. Am I lucky or what?"

"Big deal," George said. "Jessie gave us free Big Thrills passes for a week."

"How's that for lucky?" Bess asked.

Orson's eyes opened wide. "Free passes? No way!"

Bess pointed to Nancy's pocket. "They're in there."

Nancy saw Orson look at her pocket. She thought he looked jealous and a little bit angry.

"Let's go," Nancy told her friends. "I want to ride the Whizzy Whirl."

"Wait," Orson said. "You have to see my magic tricks."

"No, we don't," Jessie said.

Orson reached out and pulled a bright red flower from behind Jessie's ear.

Jessie stared at the flower. "Wow! Not bad."

Orson turned to Nancy. He began to wave his wand over her head.

"Abraca-phooey!" Orson said.

Nancy stared up at the wand. She waited for something to happen.

"Well?" Nancy asked.

"Look in your pocket." Orson giggled.

Nancy shrugged. She reached in and pulled out a slimy rubber tarantula.

"Yuck!" Nancy threw the tarantula at Jessie. The girls shrieked as they tossed the spider back and forth.

"Am I good or what?" Orson laughed as he walked away.

"Gross," Nancy said. She tossed the rubber spider into a trash can. "That thing was in the same pocket as my banana taffy."

"Make sure he didn't leave any more yucky things in your pocket," Jessie said.

Nancy carefully dipped her hand into her pocket. There were no more creepy crawlies. But then Nancy noticed something even more scary.

"Oh, no!" Nancy gasped.

"What is it, Nancy?" George asked.

"The taffy is missing," Nancy said. "And so are the passes!"

# 3

# Mis-Fortune

**N**ancy felt terrible. She had promised to take care of the passes, and now they were gone.

"Check your other pocket," Jessie said.

Nancy reached into her left-hand pocket. "They aren't in here, either," she said.

"Oh, no!" Bess moaned.

Jessie unzipped her waist-pack. "I still have mine," she said.

Nancy took a deep breath. "The passes could have fallen out of my pocket while we were walking. We have to look everywhere we went."

The girls looked all around the car-

23

ousel and asked people if they'd seen the passes. They passed Marv the Marvelous's stage. Then they stopped at Tony's Taffy Stand.

"Sorry, girls," Tony said. "I didn't find any passes."

"That's what everybody's told us." Nancy sighed. "But thanks anyway, Tony."

As Nancy and her friends walked away, they heard a voice calling to them.

Nancy looked around. She saw a woman sitting outside a red tent. The woman had silver-colored hair. The woman waved to the girls. She pointed to a sign. It read, Madame Valenska, fortune-teller. Why wait? Learn your fate!

"Maybe she can tell us where the passes are," Bess said.

"I don't believe in fortune-tellers," Jessie said.

"Come on, Jessie," Nancy said. "It's worth a try."

The girls followed Madame Valenska behind a beaded curtain.

Inside the tent was a small table and two chairs. Madame Valenska sat down in one of the chairs. "Whose fortune shall I tell first?" she asked the girls.

Nancy stepped forward. "Mine. I mean . . . maybe you can tell me about something I lost."

Madame invited Nancy to sit in the chair facing her. She waved her hands in front of Nancy's face.

"I can see your name begins with a *P*. Is it . . . Patty?"

Nancy heard Jessie begin to laugh.

"It's Nancy," Nancy said.

"Nancy, Patty—close enough," Madame said with a shrug. She took Nancy's hand and traced Nancy's palm with her index finger.

"That tickles!" Nancy giggled.

"I can see that what you lost is very valuable," Madame Valenska said.

"Can you also see where they are?" Nancy asked.

Madame Valenska's eyes twinkled.

She leaned back in her chair. "All I will say is this: Be aware. The clues are there. Be wise. And use your eyes."

Nancy wrinkled her nose. "That sounds more like a riddle than a fortune."

"It *is* a riddle," Madame said. "But it also tells your fortune."

"Thanks," Nancy said. But she felt disappointed.

"I've gotten better fortunes in cookies," Jessie whispered as they headed out of the tent.

The girls walked silently to a bench near the Rambling Rosie.

"We're never going to find our passes," Bess said as everyone sat down.

Nancy opened her hand and stared at her palm. "I wonder what Madame Valenska meant when she said 'the clues are there.' Maybe 'clues' means that I have a new mystery to solve."

"You mean, the mystery of the missing passes?" George asked Nancy.

"You're a great detective, Nancy," Jessie said. "But there are a thousand people at this fair. The passes could be anywhere. And anyone could have taken them. You would never solve this mystery."

Bess jumped up from the bench. She put her hands on her hips. "Nancy can solve any mystery—even this one."

Bess pointed to the Rambling Rosie. "And if she doesn't, she'll ride the Rambling Rosie three times in a row!"

# 4

# Daffy
# for Taffy

B ess!" Nancy cried. "Why did you make that promise?"

"Because you *will* solve the mystery," Bess said.

"And if you don't, we'll all ride the Rambling Rosie together," Jessie said. "It would be so neat!"

"Okay," Nancy said with a sigh. "I'll ride the Rambling Rosie, but only if I don't find the passes."

"You will," Bess said. "Did you bring your detective notebook?"

Nancy shook her head. "It's in my room. I'll have to wait until I go home."

"Can we come over and help?" Jessie said. "If we all get permission, that is."

"Sure," Nancy said. "I can use all the help I can get."

"You'll find the passes," George said. "But let's go on some more rides. Just in case it's our last day."

The girls went on one more ride. Then they played the ring toss game. They even watched Coconut play peek-aboo with a little boy. Then they met Mrs. Shapiro.

On the ride to Nancy's house, everyone told Mrs. Shapiro about the rides they had gone on. But all Nancy could think about was the missing passes. She couldn't wait to open her notebook and get to work.

When they reached Nancy's house, Bess and George called their mothers and got permission to stay for a while. Then everyone went upstairs to Nancy's room.

All the girls sat on the rug beside Nancy's bed. Bess held a stuffed cat she'd won at the ring toss game.

"Isn't she beautiful?" Bess asked. She combed the cat's long pink hair. "I'm going to call her Pretty Kitty."

"I wish you had picked the stuffed soccer ball," George said. "Now, that was neat."

Jessie stared at Bess and George. "Sometimes I can't believe you're cousins. You two are so different."

Nancy opened her notebook. She turned to a clean page. She wrote: "Missing: Passes to Big Thrills." Under that she wrote: "List of Suspects."

"Who's first?" Jessie asked. She was looking over Nancy's shoulder.

"Rebecca Ramirez," Nancy said. She wrote down Rebecca's name. "She looked upset when she found out Jessie gave us the free passes instead of her."

"She also knew that the passes were in your pocket," Bess added.

"Then she ran away before the carousel ride began," Nancy said. She wrote everything down in her notebook.

"I've known Rebecca since kinder-

garten," Jessie said. "Even though we had a fight, we're still friends. Besides, she'd never steal anything."

"My dad says that even friends can make mistakes," Nancy told Jessie.

Nancy's father, Carson Drew, was a lawyer. He often helped Nancy with her cases.

Nancy thought for a moment. "My next suspect," she said, "is Orson Wong."

"Yeah," George said. "Did you see the weird look on Orson's face when he found out about the passes?"

"Orson *always* has a weird look on his face," Jessie said.

"If Orson could make a tarantula appear in my pocket," Nancy said, "maybe he could make the passes disappear."

"Into his *own* pocket," George said.

Nancy added Orson's name to her list.

"I should have bought some taffy at the fair today," George said. "I could go for some now."

"I had a whole bag in my pocket before it was stolen," Nancy said sadly.

"Whoever stole the free passes," Jessie said, "must like taffy, too."

Nancy sat up straight. "Coconut!"

"Nah. I like chocolate," Jessie said.

"No, no, no," Nancy said. "I mean Coconut the Peekaboo Chimp. His trainer told me Coconut loves taffy. Maybe he took the passes."

"Why would a chimp want passes to a fair?" George said.

"Coconut reached in my pocket for the taffy," Nancy said. "When he did that, he might have accidentally pulled out the passes, too."

"Where would he have put them?" Jessie asked.

Nancy snapped her fingers. "Coconut was wearing overalls with huge pockets."

Bess shook her finger. "I knew that smelly chimp was up to no good."

"Coconut didn't smell," Nancy insisted. "And he's still just a suspect. Just like Orson and Rebecca."

"Yeah, but a whole lot hairier."
George laughed.

Nancy leaned against her bed.

"I wish we could go to the fair tomorrow and do some investigating," she said.

"How are we going to do that without our passes?" George asked.

"I know," Nancy said. "Hannah offered to take us to Big Thrills this year as a treat. Maybe tomorrow could be the day."

Hannah Gruen worked as the Drews' housekeeper.

"I still have my pass," Jessie said. "So I can go with you tomorrow."

The girls gave each other high-fives. Then George looked at her watch. "We'd better go home," she said. "It's almost dinnertime."

Nancy walked her friends outside. Suddenly she heard two boys yell out.

"Look out!"

"Beep! Beep!"

Nancy froze. The boys were speeding down the sidewalk on roller skates.

Bess and George backed up against a tree. Jessie and Nancy ran for the curb.

"Watch where you're going!" George shouted as the boys screeched to a stop.

Nancy recognized them. They were Lonny and Lenny Wong, Orson's brothers. They were six years old, and they were twins.

Lenny pointed to the pin on Nancy's jacket. "Hey! Isn't that Coconut the Peekaboo Chimp?" he asked.

Nancy nodded. "Did you ever meet Coconut?" she asked the boys.

"Nope," Lonny said. "But maybe we'll see him tomorrow."

"Orson is taking us to Big Thrills for the whole day," Lenny said.

"We saw Orson there today," Nancy said. "Is he going to be at Big Thrills tomorrow, too?"

"Why?" Lonny asked with a silly grin. "Do you like him?"

Lenny made sloppy kissing noises. The twins laughed as they skated away.

"Is Orson going to be there or not?" George yelled after them.

"You bet," Lenny called over his shoulder. "He just got three free passes!"

The girls stared at one another.

"Did he say—" Bess started to say.

"Yup," Nancy said. "Three free passes."

# 5

# Pocket Full
# of Trouble

**N**ancy could hardly sleep a wink that night. When Sunday morning finally came, Hannah drove Nancy, Bess, George, and Jessie to Big Thrills.

"Thanks for taking us, Hannah," Nancy said as they pulled into the parking lot.

"This is as much fun for me as it is for you," Hannah said. "I haven't eaten cotton candy in years."

Just then Bess grabbed Nancy's arm. "There's Orson Wong," she whispered.

Orson was walking toward the gate with his father and brothers. The three boys were waving pink passes with orange borders in the air.

"We have free passes! We have free passes!" Orson sang as he followed his father to the ticket taker.

Nancy took her notebook out of her jacket pocket. Under her list of suspects she wrote: "Orson—three free passes. They look just like ours."

"Okay, girls," Hannah said as they walked inside. "What ride should we go on first?"

"Um . . . Hannah?" Nancy asked. "Would you mind if we did something else right now?"

"Like solve a mystery?" Hannah chuckled. "I thought you were on a new case when I saw that blue notebook."

"Can we? Please?" Nancy asked.

Hannah tilted her head. "Well, as long as you check in with me every hour. We can meet at the balloon stand."

"You're neat, Hannah!" Nancy said.

"Thanks," Hannah said. "Now if

you'll excuse me, I simply *must* ride the Curly Caterpillar."

After Hannah left, Nancy turned to her friends. "Let's follow Orson first. Then we'll look for Coconut."

"I think I'd rather go on the Curly Caterpillar with Hannah," Jessie said.

"That's okay, Jessie," Nancy said. "Go catch up to her. We can meet you later."

"And if you don't solve the case by the time the fair closes, you'll—" Jessie started to say.

"I know, I know." Nancy sighed. "I'll have to ride the Rambling Rosie."

"There's Mr. Wong," George said after Jessie ran to catch up with Hannah.

Orson's father was sitting on a bench. He was loading a video camera. The twins were watching a clown make balloon animals.

"Where's Orson?" Bess asked.

"There he is," Nancy said. "He's walking toward the Barrel of Monkeys."

The Barrel of Monkeys ride was shaped like a giant wooden barrel. People stood inside it as it spun faster and faster.

The girls stopped at a sign outside the ramp. It read, Warning: Empty your pockets before going on this ride.

"I guess one of us should stay outside and hold our things," Nancy said.

"I'll do it," Bess offered happily.

"You'll do *anything* to get out of this ride, Bess." George laughed.

After they emptied their pockets into Bess's hands, Nancy saw Orson staring at the sign. He looked both ways before dashing up the ramp.

"Orson isn't emptying his pockets," Nancy said angrily.

Nancy and George entered the giant barrel. They strapped themselves in across from Orson.

A voice came over the loudspeaker. "Is everybody ready?" it said. "Then here we go-go-go!"

The barrel began to spin. Nancy held on, but she didn't have to. The barrel spun so fast that everyone stuck to the sides.

"It's going faster!" Nancy shouted happily.

Then the barrel tilted. "This is the best part!" George cried.

Suddenly, all sorts of things started flying around inside the barrel. Nancy saw baseball cards and a few sticks of gum fly by. Then she saw pieces of pink-and-orange paper floating in the air.

The passes! Nancy thought with a gasp.

The ride came to a stop. Everything that had been flying around floated to the bottom of the barrel.

"Who do these things belong to?" the ride operator asked sternly.

Orson unstrapped himself and ran forward. "Me. They fell out of my pocket."

"You were supposed to empty your pockets," the man scolded.

"I'm sorry," Orson said. "I just had some things that I didn't want to lose."

"Orson, may I have those passes, please?" Nancy asked in a firm voice.

Orson stared at Nancy. "No way!" he shouted. He hurried off the ride. Nancy, Bess, and George followed.

The girls chased Orson all the way to Marv the Magician's stage. Lonny and Lenny were there, chomping on cotton candy. Their father stood nearby, filming everything.

Just then Marv walked over. He was carrying a silver cape. "What's going on, kids?" he asked.

George pointed to Orson. "The assistant you picked yesterday might be a thief!"

Nancy explained everything about the missing passes to Marv. She even told him about the rubber spider.

Marv threw his head back and laughed. "Orson slipped that spider in your pocket while you were watching the wand. Right, Orson?" he asked.

"Yes," Orson admitted. "But that trick is supposed to be a secret."

"Then it's *our* little secret," Marv said with a friendly wink.

"Well, that explains the spider," Nancy said. "But how did Orson get three free passes?"

"From me," Marv said.

"From you?" Nancy asked.

"I gave them to Orson for being such a great assistant," Marv said. Then he draped the silver cape around Orson's shoulders.

Lonny and Lenny smiled proudly.

"Nyah, nyah, nyah!" Orson sneered. Then he showed the passes to Nancy.

"These passes are good from Sunday to Sunday," Nancy whispered to George.

"Ours were good from Saturday to Saturday," George said.

"Sorry," Nancy said. She handed Orson the tickets.

"That's okay," Orson said. He grinned and waved his wand. "And now . . . Orson the Awesome is going to turn you all into lizards. Abraca-dopey, canta-lopey!"

Nancy, Bess, and George screamed and ran away.

"Orson is no longer a suspect," Nancy said. Nancy, Bess, and George were at the snack stand. Nancy opened her notebook and crossed Orson's name off the suspect list.

"That leaves us with Rebecca and Coconut," George said. She took a long sip of her blueberry smoothie.

Nancy checked her watch and gulped. There were only a couple of hours left before she might have to ride the Rambling Rosie.

"What time is it, Nancy?" Bess asked.

"Time to meet Hannah," Nancy said.

The girls joined Hannah and Jessie at the balloon stand. Everyone rode on the Loopy Loop and the mini train. Then Hannah and Jessie headed for the fun house.

"Let's get some taffy," George said to Nancy and Bess.

When they got to Tony's stand, George bought a bag of vanilla. Bess wanted to try the kiwi-flavored taffy. Then it was Nancy's turn.

"I'll have a bag of banana taffy, please," she told Tony.

"I was afraid of that," Tony said.

"Why, Tony?" Nancy asked.

"Someone got into my taffy truck early last night," Tony explained. "The banana taffy boxes were ripped open."

Nancy stared at Tony. "You mean—"

Tony nodded. "Almost all of my banana taffy was stolen!"

# 6

# Monkey Business

**W**ho do you think did it?" Nancy asked.

"I'm not sure," Tony said. He glared at Nancy's Coconut pin. "But I think I have a pretty good idea."

"Coconut?" Bess gasped.

"He did it once before," Tony said. "We found the taffy in his trailer."

"Tony," Nancy said. "Could you tell us where Coconut's trailer is?"

"Sure," Tony said. He pointed to the parking lot at the other side of the fair. Nancy could see some trailers parked in a neat row.

"It sounds like Coconut might have taken Tony's taffy," Nancy said to Bess and George as they walked toward the trailers. "He also might have stolen *my* taffy."

"And the passes," George said.

Nancy stopped walking. She wrote "stolen taffy" under her list of clues.

The girls reached the row of trailers. "That one has a sign on the door," Nancy said. She stepped closer. "It says, Coconut the Peekaboo Chimp."

Nancy peeked in through the screen door.

"What do you see?" George asked.

"There's a small couch, a bucket of bananas, a cage," Nancy whispered. "And—wow!"

"Wow what?" George asked.

"The overalls that Coconut wore yesterday are lying on the cage," Nancy said. "I want to look inside the pockets."

Nancy turned the doorknob. "It's open," she whispered to Bess and George.

"Don't go in there," Bess said.

"I'm just going to take a quick peek," Nancy said. She tiptoed inside.

Nancy reached for the overalls. "I feel something," she said. She reached into a pocket. Then she pulled out a small plastic bag. "It's banana taffy!"

"Are our passes there, too?" George asked. She crossed her fingers as she and Bess entered the trailer.

Nancy checked both pockets. "Nope. No passes," she said sadly.

Bess sat down on the couch. "Yuck. This couch smells like bananas. And it's lumpy, too."

"Lumpy?" Nancy asked. She walked over to the couch. She lifted a cushion. Then she gasped.

"Pieces of taffy—banana taffy!" she cried. "Tony was right. Coconut *is* the taffy thief."

"Eek, eek, eek!" came a sound from outside the trailer.

"I think someone's coming," Nancy whispered. "We're trapped."

Just then Barbara Woodhall marched into the trailer. Coconut was close behind her. "What are you girls doing in Coconut's trailer?" Ms. Woodhall asked angrily.

Nancy told Ms. Woodhall all about the missing passes.

"Did you find them in here?" Ms. Woodhall asked. She looked worried.

"All we found was taffy," Nancy said.

"Stolen taffy," George added.

Ms. Woodhall's mouth dropped open. Then Tony marched into the trailer.

"Ms. Woodhall," Tony said. "I want to speak to you about your chimp."

"Coconut?" Ms. Woodhall turned to the chimp. "Did you take Tony's taffy?"

Coconut covered his face with his hands.

"But he went to chimp school," Ms. Woodhall told Tony.

"I guess he didn't do his homework," Tony said angrily.

"I left Coconut alone only once. It was early last night," Ms. Woodhall said.

Nancy turned to Tony. "Didn't you

say your taffy was stolen early last night?"

"My truck was parked right outside this trailer," Tony said. "The chimp must have sneaked in when I wasn't looking."

"I'm sorry, Tony," Ms. Woodhall said. "If Coconut could talk, he would apologize to you."

"Yeah, sure," Tony mumbled.

Nancy watched Tony gather his taffy. Then he left to go back to the taffy stand.

Ms. Woodhall invited the girls to search the trailer for the missing passes. The girls looked everywhere, but they didn't find the passes.

"It looks as if Coconut took just my taffy," Nancy said, "not the passes."

Coconut walked over to Bess. He reached out and gently shook her hand. Bess giggled. "Oh, he's sweet. Maybe Coconut isn't so bad, after all."

Nancy took out her notebook. She crossed Coconut's name off the suspect list. Then she and her friends left the trailer and walked back to the fair.

"Now the only suspect left is Rebecca," Nancy said.

"Speaking of Rebecca," George said, "look who's at the Squirting Gallery."

"Rebecca Ramirez," Nancy said. "With Amara Shane and Emily Reeves."

Rebecca, Amara, and Emily were getting ready to knock over plastic bottles with water pistols.

Suddenly Nancy saw something that made her heart jump.

Sticking out of Rebecca's jeans pocket was something pink and orange!

"Bess, George, look!" Nancy said. "Those could be our passes!"

# 7

# Ladybug, Ladybug

**N**ancy walked up to Rebecca. She reached out and tapped her on the shoulder.

Rebecca spun around with the water pistol in her hand. She squirted Nancy right in the face!

"Yuck!" Nancy sputtered as the water gushed into her mouth.

"Why were you sneaking up on me, Nancy Drew?" Rebecca demanded.

Nancy spit out the water. Amara stared with surprise. Emily giggled.

"You ruined my chance of winning the ladybug pajama bag!" Rebecca cried. She pointed to a stuffed ladybug hanging with the other prizes.

"I'm sorry," Nancy said. "But—"

Rebecca put the water pistol down with a clunk. Then she turned to Amara and Emily. "I want to go home right now!"

Amara and Emily waved goodbye as they hurried after Rebecca.

Just then Nancy heard someone call her name. It was Jessie.

"The fair is closing in about an hour, Nancy," Jessie said. "Have you found the passes yet?"

Nancy froze. She shook her head.

"Then it's Rambling Rosie time," Jessie cried. "Yee-haw!"

"Wait, Jessie," Nancy said.

"For what?" Jessie asked.

"I just found a clue in Rebecca's back pocket. It might be the passes," Nancy said.

"I saw them, too," George said.

"They were pink and orange," Bess said.

"So what?" Jessie said. "They could have been orange lollipops. Or pink sunglasses."

"You just want me to ride the Rambling Rosie," Nancy said with a frown.

"Come on." Jessie groaned. "We made a deal, remember?"

Nancy made a face. "How can I forget?"

"This is all my fault," Bess said. "I'm sorry I told Jessie you'd ride the Rambling Rosie, Nancy."

"That's okay." Nancy told Bess. "You can hold my notebook while I go on the ride."

"Don't worry, Nancy," George said, patting her back. "It'll be a blast."

That's what *you* say, Nancy thought.

On their way to the roller coaster, Nancy saw Madame Valenska sitting outside her tent. She smiled and waved to the girls.

"What did she say?" Nancy whispered to herself. " 'Be aware. The clues are there. Be wise. And use your eyes.' "

At the gate outside the Rambling Rosie, Nancy handed her notebook to Bess.

"Do you have anything else in your pockets?" Bess asked while Jessie and George ran to the line.

"Let me see," Nancy said. She dug inside both pockets. Suddenly she felt something stuck inside her right pocket.

Nancy wiggled her fingers and pulled out a shiny red object. It was a ring— a ladybug ring.

"This isn't mine," Nancy said, holding up the ring. "Whose could it be?"

"Be aware. The clues are there. Be wise. And use your eyes." The words swirled around in Nancy's mind.

"Rebecca!" Nancy cried. "She said she loves ladybugs."

Then Nancy waved her arms in the air. "Jessie, George! Look what I found!"

"Did you find the passes?" Jessie asked as she and George hurried over.

"No," Nancy said. She held up the ring. "But I did find this."

"Nancy thinks it might belong to Rebecca Ramirez," Bess said.

"If it *is* Rebecca's, she might have dropped it in my pocket when she reached for the passes," Nancy said.

"When do you think she did that?" George asked.

Nancy thought for a second. "Rebecca helped me climb up on the carousel horse. She put her hands around my waist to help me up."

Nancy's eyes lit up. "I want to talk to Rebecca right away."

"Forget it," George said. "They're probably almost home by now."

"Then I'll speak to her tomorrow," Nancy said.

"Tomorrow?" Jessie said. "But what about the Rambling Rosie?"

"All I need is just one more day, Jessie," Nancy said. "One more day."

That evening Nancy ate dinner with her father.

"How is your case coming along, Pudding Pie," Carson Drew asked.

"So far so good, Daddy," Nancy said.

She took a sip of milk. Then she told her father all about the ladybug ring.

"I'm still not sure it belongs to Rebecca," Nancy said. "But it's still a great clue."

"And if it helps you solve the mystery," Carson said, "then it's one lucky ladybug."

Nancy sighed. "Maybe for me, Daddy. But not for Rebecca."

On Monday afternoon Nancy met Bess and George on Rebecca's block.

"Why didn't Jessie come, too?" George asked.

"When I spoke to her on the phone, she said she still didn't want to talk to Rebecca," Nancy explained.

"Jessie is being so stubborn," Bess said.

The girls were almost at the Ramirezes' house.

"Remember," George said in a low voice, "Rebecca is a good actress, so she might act innocent."

Nancy rang the doorbell. After a

minute Rebecca opened the door. She was wearing dangling ladybug earrings.

"H-hi," Rebecca said.

Nancy thought Rebecca looked surprised to see them. And a little nervous.

"Hi, Rebecca," Nancy said. "Your earrings are so cool. What other ladybug things do you have?"

Rebecca smiled proudly. "I have a ladybug umbrella, a ladybug nightshirt, a ladybug ring—"

Nancy took the ring out of her pocket. She held it in front of Rebecca's face.

"You mean like this one?" Nancy asked.

# 8

## Nancy Goes for It

**M**y ladybug ring," Rebecca whispered. Then she looked up. "I mean—what a neat ladybug ring!"

"I found it inside *my* pocket," Nancy told Rebecca.

Rebecca smiled and shook her head. "My ladybug ring was different. It was blue."

"Who ever heard of a blue ladybug?" George said.

"Besides," Rebecca went on, "that ring could belong to anybody. Ladybugs are very popular this year."

"But, Rebecca," Nancy said, "your hands were around my waist when you helped me climb on to the carousel horse. Remember?"

Rebecca began to close the door. "I've got to clean my room. I hope you find your missing passes."

"Wait a minute!" Nancy called. She reached out and kept the door from closing. "Rebecca, I never told you the passes were missing. How did you know?"

Rebecca stared at Nancy. "Jessie told me last night," she said quickly.

"Jessie hasn't spoken to you for a week," Nancy said.

Rebecca looked down and didn't say anything.

"Did you take our free passes, Rebecca?" Nancy asked softly.

Rebecca took a deep breath. Then she nodded. "I was mad that Jessie gave you free passes and not me."

"But that didn't mean you had to steal them," Nancy said.

"I know and I felt really bad," Rebecca said. "I wanted to give them back to you on Saturday night."

"Why didn't you?" Nancy asked.

"Because I had already promised Amara and Emily free passes for Sunday," Rebecca explained. "They had no idea they were . . . taken."

"You mean *stolen*," George said.

"I was going to give them back to you today," Rebecca said. "Honest!"

"Today is here," Nancy said. She held out her hand. "Can we please have our passes back, Rebecca?"

"Sure," Rebecca said. "They're upstairs in my jeans pocket—"

Nancy saw Rebecca gasp and put her hands to her mouth.

"What's up, Rebecca?" Bess asked.

"My jeans are in the wash right now!" Rebecca wailed.

"The wash?" Nancy said.

The girls ran downstairs to the Ramirezes' laundry room.

Mrs. Ramirez stopped the dryer. "I told you to empty your pockets before putting your clothes in the hamper, Rebecca," Mrs. Ramirez said. She handed Rebecca her jeans.

Nancy could see that the jeans were still damp when Rebecca stuck her hand inside the pocket.

"Uh-oh," Rebecca said.

"What?" Nancy cried.

Rebecca pulled out three soggy pink and orange passes.

"The ink is all blurry," Nancy said.

"I'm sorry," Rebecca said.

"You should be," George said. "The passes are totally ruined."

"Maybe they're not," Nancy said. "Let's show them to Mrs. Shapiro."

George turned to Rebecca. "You should come, too. You have to tell her what happened."

Rebecca rolled her eyes. "Oh, great. Now Jessie *really* won't talk to me."

The girls walked the few blocks to Jessie's house.

Nancy rang the bell. After a minute, Mrs. Shapiro opened the door.

"Hi, girls," Mrs. Shapiro said. "Did you come to see Jessie?"

"We really came to see you," Nancy

said. She held up the soggy passes. "You see, the passes had a little accident."

"I'll say!" Mrs. Shapiro said. "Come inside and tell me what happened."

Mrs. Shapiro led the girls into the living room. After everyone sat down, Rebecca explained everything.

Mrs. Shapiro put her hand on Rebecca's shoulder. "Thanks for telling the truth, Rebecca," she said.

"Are the passes still good, Mrs. Shapiro?" Nancy asked.

Mrs. Shapiro flipped the passes around in her hand. "Let me make a quick phone call to find out," she said.

Rebecca fell back on the sofa next to Jessie. "She's calling the police! I know it! I'm going to jail for a million years!"

Nancy giggled. "She's probably just calling her office."

"And this isn't the school play, Rebecca," George groaned.

Jessie gave Rebecca an angry look.

"How could you do something like that?"

"I told you, Jessie," Rebecca said. "I was mad at you."

"Oh, yeah?" Jessie said. "Well, I was mad that you took Amara Shane on your family picnic last week instead of me."

"We took Amara because her parents asked us to," Rebecca said. "They had some grown-up party to go to that day."

Jessie stared at Rebecca. "Really?"

Rebecca nodded. "I like Amara. But I really wanted to take you. There just wasn't any more room in the car."

"You should have told me," Jessie said.

"How could I?" Rebecca cried. "You wouldn't talk to me all week!"

"Oh . . . right," Jessie said slowly.

Mrs. Shapiro walked back into the living room. "Great news, girls," she said. "The passes are fine."

"Yay!" Nancy cheered.

"And guess what?" Mrs. Shapiro

asked. "A woman at work offered me another free ticket."

"Double-yay!" Nancy cried.

"Who are you going to give the extra pass to, Jessie?" Bess asked.

Jessie turned to Rebecca and smiled. "Would you like it, Rebecca?"

Rebecca's face lit up. "Do ladybugs fly? You bet I would!"

George turned to Nancy. "You did it again, Nancy. You solved the mystery."

"Now you won't have to ride the Rambling Rosie," Bess said. "Right?"

Nancy didn't answer. She just smiled.

Later that afternoon Mrs. Shapiro took all five girls to Big Thrills.

"What ride should we go on first?" Rebecca asked when they were inside.

"How about the Rambling Rosie?" Nancy asked.

"Are you sure, Nancy?" George asked.

"Do ladybugs fly?" Nancy laughed.

In just a few minutes, Nancy was riding the fastest, biggest ride at Big Thrills.

"Here comes the scariest part!" Jessie shouted as the Rambling Rosie rumbled to the top of the highest peak.

The Rambling Rosie stopped at the top for a few seconds. Then it roared down the tracks at top speed.

"Way-to-gooooo!" Nancy screamed. She waved her arms in the air. She felt as if she were flying.

When the ride stopped, Bess ran over. "How do you feel, Nancy?" she asked.

Nancy gave her friends the thumbs-up sign. "I feel . . . awesome!"

That evening before dinner, Nancy curled up on a chair in the den. She took out her notebook and opened it to a blank page. Then she began to write:

Guess what? Today I rode the Rambling Rosie, and not because I didn't solve the case. I did that, too!

Madame Valenska was right. The

clues were there—if you just looked hard enough.

Madame is a great fortune-teller. I wonder if she was ever a detective, too.

Case closed.

# BRAND-NEW SERIES!
## Meet up with suspense and mystery in

**FRANK AND JOE HARDY: THE CLUES BROTHERS™**

# #1 The Gross Ghost Mystery
Frank and Joe are making friends and meeting monsters!

# #2 The Karate Clue
Somebody's kicking up a major mess!

# #3 First Day, Worst Day
Everybody's mad at Joe! Is he a tattletale?

# #4 Jump Shot Detectives
He shoots! He scores! He steals?

# #5 Dinosaur Disaster
It's big, it's bad, it's a Bayport-asaurus! Sort-of.

## By Franklin W. Dixon
Look for a brand-new story every other month
at your local bookseller

A MINSTREL® BOOK

**Published by Pocket Books**

1398-04

**Do your younger brothers and sisters
want to read books like yours?**

Let them know there are books just for them!

# THE NANCY DREW NOTEBOOKS®

**Look for a brand-new story every other month**

Available from Minstrel® Books
Published by Pocket Books

1356-01

# TAKE A RIDE
# WITH THE KIDS ON BUS FIVE!

Natalie Adams and James Penny have just started
third grade. They like their teacher, and they like
Maple Street School. The only trouble is, they have
to ride bad old Bus Five to get there!

### #1 THE BAD NEWS BULLY
Can Natalie and James stop the bully on Bus Five?

### #2 WILD MAN AT THE WHEEL
When Mr. Balter calls in sick,
the kids get some strange new drivers.

### #3 FINDERS KEEPERS
The kids on Bus Five keep losing things.
Is there a thief on board?

### #4 I SURVIVED ON BUS FIVE
Bad luck turns into big fun
when Bus Five breaks down in a rainstorm.

## BY MARCIA LEONARD
## ILLUSTRATED BY JULIE DURRELL

A MINSTREL® BOOK
Published by Pocket Books

1237-04

# FULL HOUSE™
# Michelle

A MINSTREL® BOOK
Published by Pocket Books

**Simon & Schuster Mail Order Dept. BWB**
**200 Old Tappan Rd., Old Tappan, N.J. 07675**

Please send me the books I have checked above. I am enclosing $_____(please add $0.75 to cover the
postage and handling for each order. Please add appropriate sales tax). Send check or money order--no cash or C.O.D.'s please. Allow up to
six weeks for delivery. For purchase over $10.00 you may use VISA: card number, expiration date and customer signature must be included.

Name _____

Address _____

City _____ State/Zip _____

VISA Card # _____ Exp.Date _____

Signature _____

1033-26